# THE ADVENTURES
# OF BENNY AND WATCH
# MEET THE BOXCAR CHILDREN

You will also want to read:
## A Present for Grandfather
## Benny's New Friend
## The Magic Show Mystery
## Benny Goes Into Business
## Watch Runs Away
## The Secret Under the Tree
## Benny's Saturday Surprise
## Sam Makes Trouble
## Watch, the Superdog!

Library of Congress Cataloging-in-Publication Data

Warner, Gertrude Chandler, 1890-1979
Meet the Boxcar Children / created by Gertrude Chandler Warner;
illustrated by Daniel Mark Duffy.
p.   cm.
Summary: Four orphaned children make a home for themselves
in an abandoned boxcar and are united with their grandfather.
ISBN 0-8075-5034-5
[1. Brothers and sisters—Fiction. 2. Orphans—Fiction. 3.Grandfathers—Fiction.]
I. Duffy, Daniel M., ill.  II. Title.
PZ7.W244Me      1998
[Fic]--dc21      98-6196
CIP
AC

Copyright © 1998 by Albert Whitman & Company.
Published in 1998 by Albert Whitman & Company,
6340 Oakton Street, Morton Grove, Illinois 60053.
Published simultaneously in Canada by
Fitzhenry & Whiteside, Markham, Ontario.

# The Adventures of Benny and Watch ™

## MEET THE BOXCAR CHILDREN

Created by **Gertrude Chandler Warner**

Illustrated by **Daniel Mark Duffy**

Albert Whitman & Company

Morton Grove, Illinois

Four children stood in front of a bakery. They were very hungry and tired.

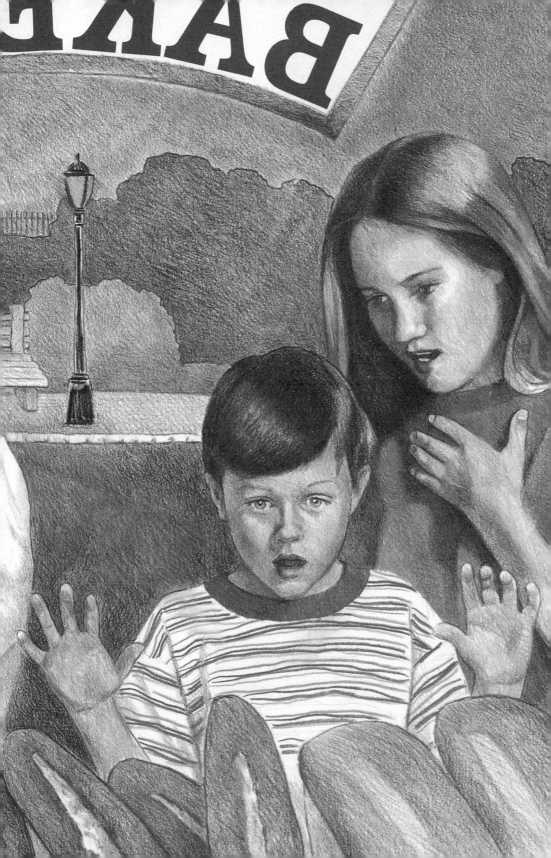

The baker's wife came out and gave them some bread.

"Where are your parents?" she asked.

"We are orphans," said Henry sadly. He was the oldest child.

Benny was the youngest. "We have a grandfather," he said. "But we've never seen him. We think he doesn't like us."

The children had no place to sleep. "Can we stay here tonight?" asked Jessie, Benny's oldest sister.

"Yes," said the baker's wife.

Benny and Violet fell asleep.
But Jessie and Henry heard
the baker's wife talking to her
husband.

She wanted to send Benny
to the Children's Home. "He's
too little to keep," she said.

"We have to leave," said
Henry. So the children ran away.

In the dark night, they walked
through the woods. "We must
find a place to live," Henry said.

The moon went behind the
clouds. It started to rain.
"Where can we go?" asked Jessie.

Suddenly Jessie saw something through the trees. "A boxcar!" she cried. "We can live *there*!"

There was a big stump in front of the boxcar. Benny climbed on it. Then he stepped into the empty train car. "What a funny house," he said.

"It's warm and dry," said Jessie.
"It's our new home," Violet said.

When the rain stopped, the children went to work. They wanted to make a nice home. They found pine needles to make soft beds.

Violet found an old board.
She and Jessie made a shelf.

A stream flowed nearby,
so they had water to drink.
The children picked big, juicy
blueberries for breakfast. While
they were eating, Benny heard
a sound in the bushes.

He saw eyes watching him.
Was it a bear? No, it was a dog!

The dog held up a hurt paw.
Jessie gently pulled out a thorn.
The dog thumped his tail.
"His name is Watch," said Benny.

Benny spotted a trash dump.
"Look at all the great things
people threw away," he said.
Henry found a hammer.

Violet found plates
and spoons.

Jessie found a pot.

Benny found a cracked
pink cup. "Now I have
something to drink from,"
he said.

In the boxcar, Jessie set
the new dishes on the shelf.

Violet picked some flowers. She and Benny put the flowers in his new cup. "It's *almost* like home," he said.

Every day Henry went into town. He worked for a man named Dr. Moore.

Henry cut Dr. Moore's grass and cleaned out his garage.

He earned enough money
for milk and bread.

Dr. Moore had a lot of cherry trees.
Henry, Violet, and Jessie picked cherries
for him. Benny just ate the cherries.
Benny *loved* to eat!

One night, Dr. Moore read an ad
in the newspaper. It said:

**LOST**

Four children. Two boys and
two girls. Reward to anyone
who finds my grandchildren.
James Henry Alden

Dr. Moore knew who those four
children were. Now he knew their
grandfather was looking for them.
But he didn't tell.

Every day, the children ate and slept and played with Watch. Sometimes they played hide-and-seek.

Benny thought living in the
boxcar was fun, like camping out.
But it still wasn't quite like home.

One day Dr. Moore took Henry
to the big race in town. Henry ran
faster than the other boys and
won! A kind man gave Henry the
prize money and a silver cup.

One awful day, Violet became very sick. Henry was frightened and ran for Dr. Moore. The doctor took Violet to his house. The other children went, too.

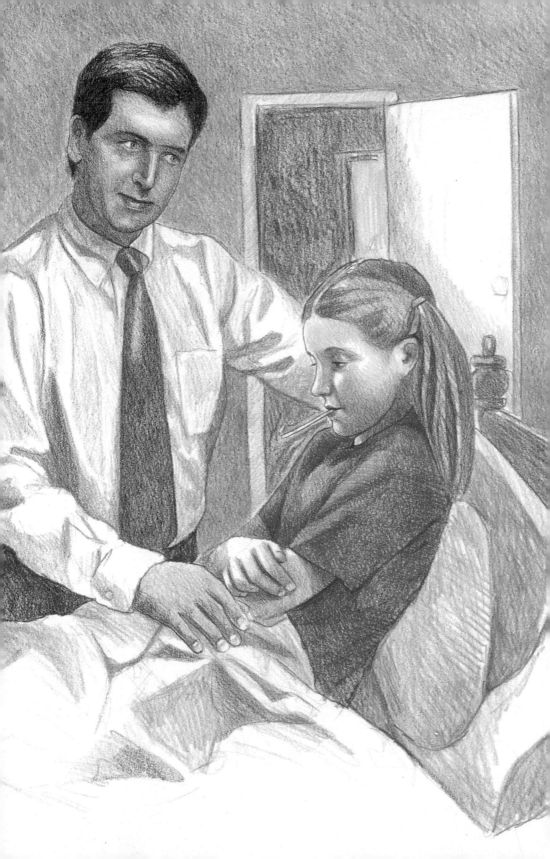

The next day, Violet was much
better. A friendly man came to see
the doctor. The man looked at
Benny. "I've lost a boy just your
age," he said.

"You can have *me*," said Benny. "I like you."

When Henry walked in, he knew he had seen the man before. "*You* gave me the prize!" he cried.

Benny was glad Grandfather
had found them. Everyone went
to live in Grandfather's big house,
even Watch.

Benny had his own room. He had a soft bed and a train set. He had a cup that wasn't cracked. "It's *almost* like home," he said. But something was missing.

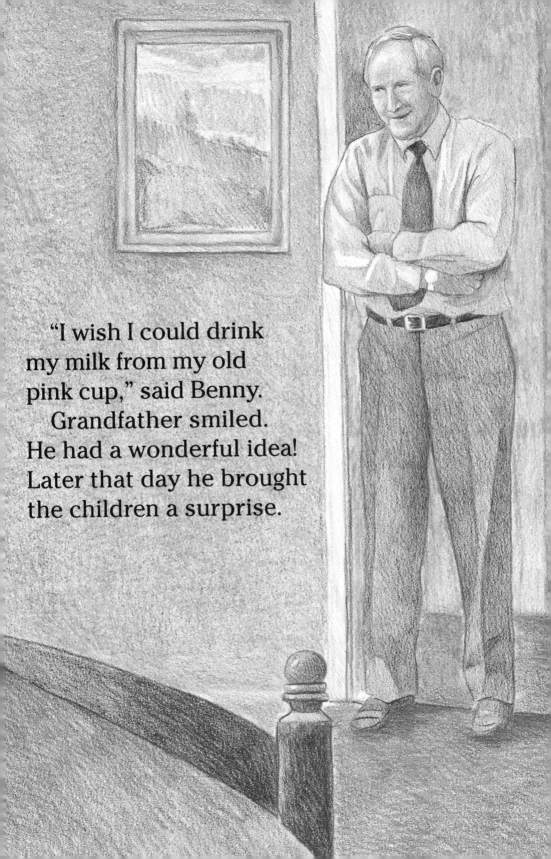

"I wish I could drink my milk from my old pink cup," said Benny. Grandfather smiled. He had a wonderful idea! Later that day he brought the children a surprise.

Their boxcar was in the backyard!
Now the children had two houses—
one old and one new. Best of all,
they had a family.

Benny gave Grandfather a big hug.
"We'll never go away from you again,"
Benny said.
And they never did.